PRINCESS IN TRAINING

Tammi Sauer

Pictures by
Joe Berger

Houghton Mifflin Harcourt
Boston   New York

For information about permission to reproduce selections from this book, write to
trade.permissions@hmhco.com or to Permissions, Houghton Mifflin Harcourt
Publishing Company, 3 Park Avenue, 19th Floor, New York, New York 10016.

www.hmhco.com

The illustrations in this book were drawn in pencil, wax crayon, and brush pen,
and colored using Photoshop.
The text type was set in Billy Serif.
The display hand-lettering was done by Leah Palmer Preiss.
The text type hand-lettering was done by Joe Berger.

The Library of Congress has cataloged the hardcover edition as follows:
Sauer, Tammi.
Princess in training / written by Tammi Sauer and illustrated by Joe Berger.
p. cm.
[1. Princesses—Fiction. 2. Individuality—Fiction. 3. Camps—Fiction. 4. Humorous stories.]
I. Berger, Joe, 1970- ill. II. Title.
PZ7.S2502Pri 2012
[E]—dc23
2011041936

ISBN: 978-0-15-206599-7 hardcover
ISBN: 978-0-544-45609-9 paperback

Manufactured in China
SCP 10 9 8 7 6 5 4 3 2

4500597913

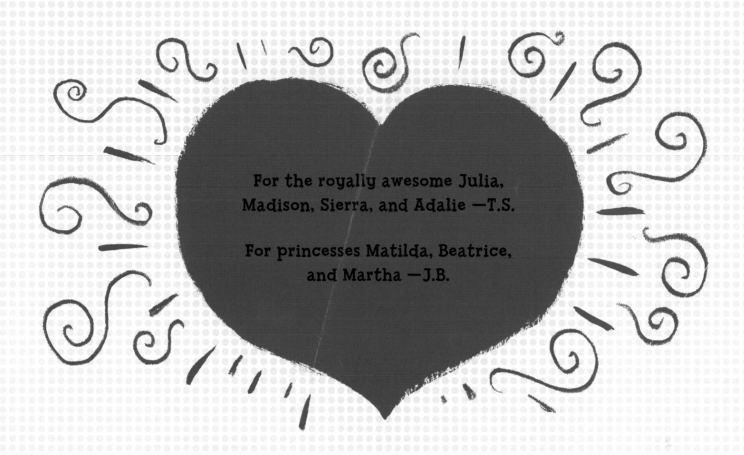

For the royally awesome Julia,
Madison, Sierra, and Adalie —T.S.

For princesses Matilda, Beatrice,
and Martha —J.B.

Viola Louise Hassenfeffer
was not an ordinary princess.

She spent her time karate-chopping,
HI-YAH!
diving into the moat,
SPLA

and skateboarding up and down the drawbridge.
SH!
ZIP!
ZUP!
ZOOM!

The kingdom was beside itself.
"You're supposed to be prim,"
said the king.
"You're supposed to be proper,"
said the queen.

Princess Viola stared at her tiara.
She was supposed to royally fit in.
She wanted to! But how would she ever
get this princess thing right?
Then one day she received a letter.

Dear Viola Louise Hassenfeffer:

Do you want to polish your princess skills? Camp Princess will teach you to wave, walk, and waltz just like royalty should. The day concludes with the Royal Bash.

Enroll now so you can be the darling of your kingdom!

Sincerely,

Madame Gertrude

Director of Camp Princess

Viola grinned.
Me? The darling
of the kingdom?

She whooshed
off to give Camp
Princess a try.

"Welcome to Camp Princess, ladies," said Madame Gertrude.
"Let's begin with the Royal Wave."

The princesses worked on good posture,
practiced proper elbow placement,
and added the customary turn of the wrist.
Princess Viola's wave was nice, but . . .

-YAH!

"Viola Louise Hassenfeffer!" called her teacher. "Royalty does not karate-chop."

"Oops." Viola ducked behind a sea of up-dos.

"Our next lesson,"
said Madame Gertrude,
"is the Frills of Fashion."

The princesses tried on gowns,
chose just the right accessories,
and learned how to walk with flair.

Princess Viola was
perfectly lovely, but . . .

she was roasting under all that taffeta.

SP

LASH!

"Viola Louise Hassenfeffer!" called her teacher. "Royalty does not dive."

"Sorry." Viola emptied her purse.

"And now," said Madame Gertrude, "Dance Lessons."

The princesses waltzed in circles, in lines, and all around the room.

Princess Viola was determined to dazzle, but . . .

she went a little overboard.

ZIP!

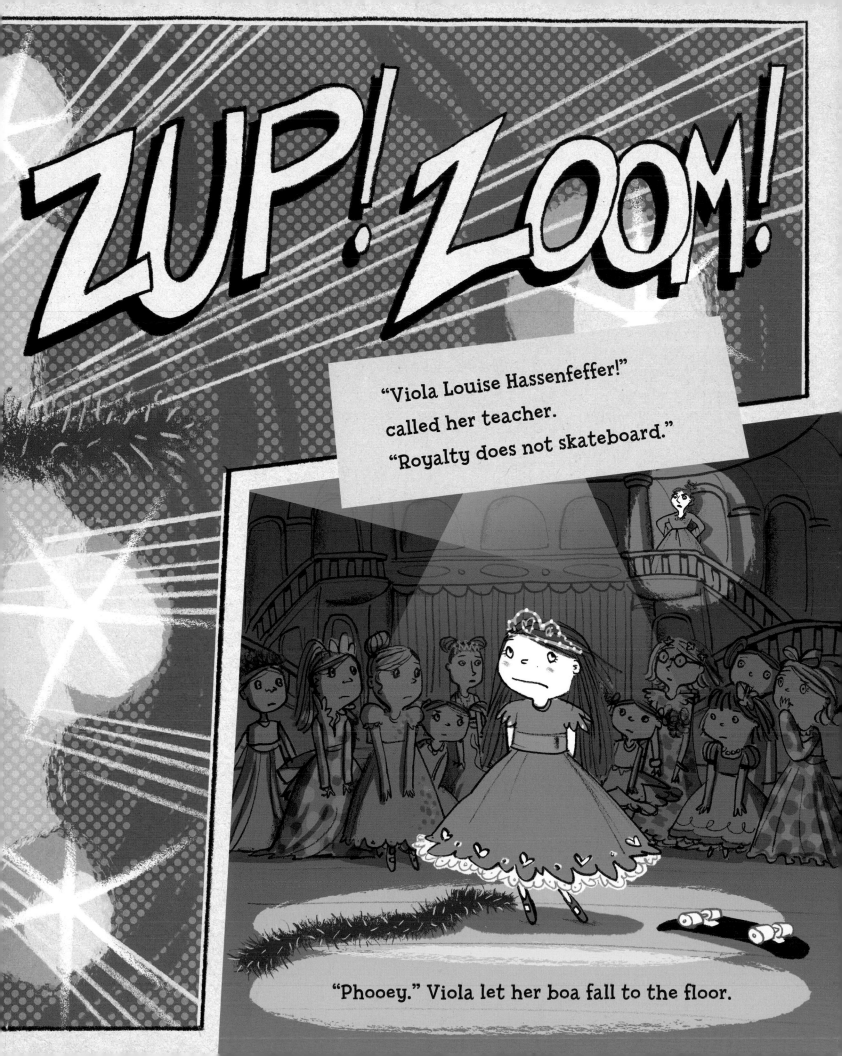

ZUP! ZOOM!

"Viola Louise Hassenfeffer!"
called her teacher.
"Royalty does not skateboard."

"Phooey." Viola let her boa fall to the floor.

Facts were facts.
Viola's day at Camp Princess was nearly
over, and she was still a royal failure.

Just then, trumpets sounded.

Madame Gertrude parted the curtains.

"Behold!" she said. "It's time for the Royal Bash!"

Every princess gasped.

"Go on," said Madame Gertrude.

"Don't be shy."

"But—" said Princess Viola.

"But *what*?"

"But there's a big green dragon behind you.
And he looks hungry!"

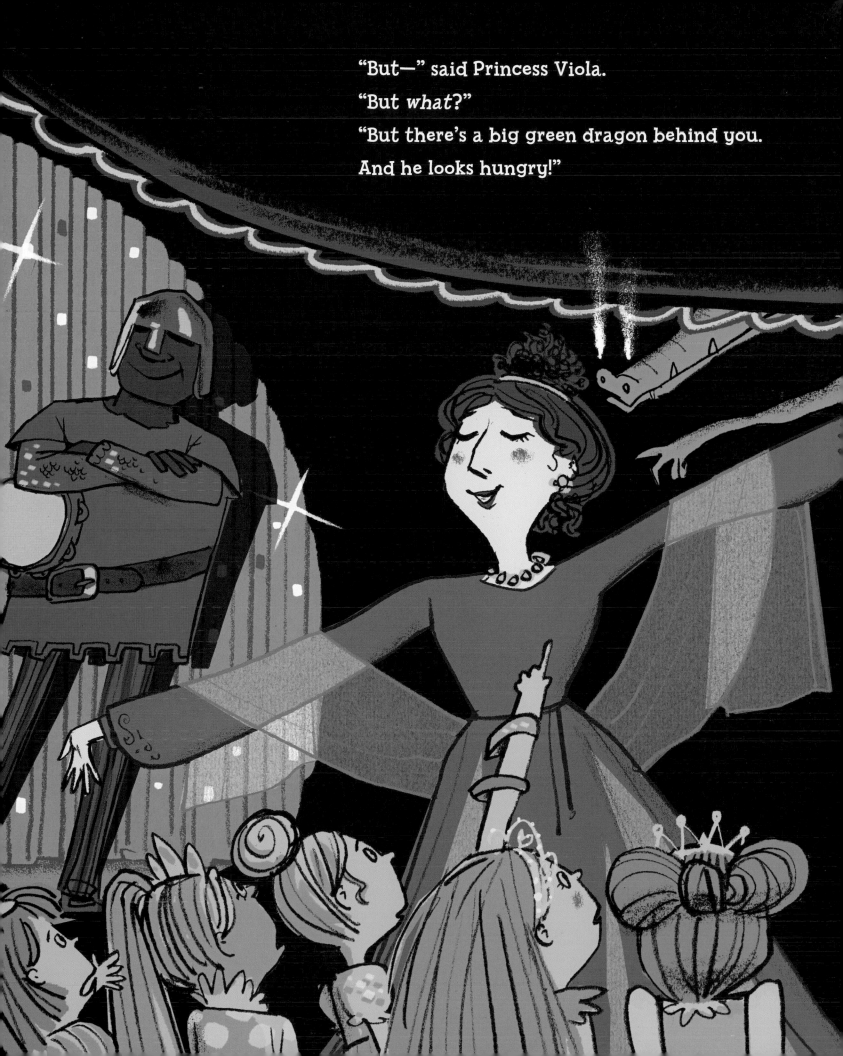

"HELP!" cried Madame Gertrude.
"SOMEONE CALL KNIGHT-1-1!"
Princesses ran here, there, and
everywhere in between.
But Viola Louise Hassenfeffer . . .

Princess Viola was a royal hero. The other princesses crowded around her.

"Well done!"

"Lovely!"

"Teach us, Viola!"

And so she did.

ZIP!

SPLASH!

ZUP!

Princess Viola wasn't prim.
She wasn't proper. But . . .

she was the darling
of her kingdom anyway.